Harry's Birthday

by Barbara Ann Porte

pictures by Yossi Abolafia

Greenwillow Books
NEW YORK

Watercolor paints and a black pen were used for the
full-color art. The text type is Plantin.

Printed in Singapore by Tien Wah Press

First Edition   10 9 8 7 6 5 4 3 2 1

Library of Congress Cataloging-in-Publication Data
Porte, Barbara Ann.
Harry's birthday / by Barbara Ann Porte;
pictures by Yossi Abolafia.
p.   cm.
Summary: Harry, who is hoping to get a cowboy
hat for his birthday, is quite surprised when he
opens all the presents at his party.
ISBN 0-688-12142-X (trade).
ISBN 0-688-12143-8 (lib. bdg.)
[1. Birthdays—Fiction.   2. Parties—Fiction.
3. Gifts—Fiction.   4. Hats—Fiction.]
I. Abolafia, Yossi, ill.   II. Title.
PZ7.P7995Haqo   1994   [E]—dc20
93-18189   CIP   AC

For Karissa Nicole Alberico
and, again, for Zachary

—B. A. P.

For Barbara Ann

—Y. A.

I, Harry, am about to have a birthday.

"My birthday's coming up.

I'm hoping for a cowboy hat,"

I tell my father.

Not for the first time, either.

"Yes," he says. "I know.

Would you like

to have a party?"

I start to say no.

I remember the last time.

I do not care to have another cake

landing in my lap.

It was an ice-cream cake.

Fortunately

I had already

blown out

all the candles.

Then I think about the presents.

Maybe this year one of them

would be a cowboy hat.

"Yes," I say.

"I'd like a party."

The next day in school
I tell Dorcas and Eddie.
"My birthday's coming up.
I'm having a party.
I'm hoping for a cowboy hat."
"Yes, I know," says Eddie.
I guess I must have mentioned it before.

"Are you having a clown?" Dorcas asks.

"The last birthday party I planned
   was ruined, all because my mother
   said, 'No clown!'"

"Ruined how?" I ask.

   Dorcas tells me.

"It was the year before we moved here.
   We still were living in Ohio.
   It was almost my birthday.
   I was planning a gala event:

   ice cream and cake,

   balloons and streamers,

games and prizes.

"The day after we sent out the invitations,
Mary Louise's arrived in the mail.
Her birthday party was the very same day
as mine and also the same time.
She was having a clown
who juggled and did magic tricks,
after which Mary Louise's mother
was taking everyone to Charlie Cheese
for pizza and pinball.

"Mary Louise's invitations had RSVP
at the bottom. So did mine.

"'Yes,' everyone RSVP'd
to Mary Louise.
'I'm sorry, but I have
a previous engagement,'
everyone RSVP'd to me.
We had to call
my party off.
Instead, that day I watched
a juggling clown
do magic tricks
and went with Mary Louise
to Charlie Cheese
for pizza and pinball.
I had a very nice time.
The only bad part was that
Mary Louise got all the presents."

That night I discuss my party
with my father.
"Can I have a clown?" I ask.
"A clown?" he says. "I don't think so."
I tell him what Dorcas told me.
"I see," he says,
and turns on the television news.

I wait for a commercial.

"If we take everyone
    to Charlie Cheese for pizza,
    I guess we can do without a clown,"
    I say.
My father says, "Harry, please.
We're planning a birthday party
    at home, not a three-ring circus."

The next day, after school,

I visit my Aunt Rose and Uncle Leo,

also my dog, Girl, who lives with them

because my father is allergic.

"My birthday's coming up," I say.

"I'm having a party—

a clownless party, with no pizza.

But I'm still hoping

for a cowboy hat."

"I know," says Aunt Rose.

She's probably been talking to my father.

"Believe me, Harry," she adds,
"there are worse things in life than
a clownless party, without pizza.
When I was your age, I was glad
just to have ice cream and cake.
It was heaven when someone
remembered the candles.
When I blew mine out,
I always wished to have
such a nice party the next year.

"When your father was your age,
   just having a birthday cake
   almost turned into a disaster."
"Really?" I say. "What happened?"
   Aunt Rose tells me.

"Cakes, in those days, came decorated
   with more than just flowers and writing.
   Sometimes lovely silver beads
   were sprinkled on the icing.
   The beads probably were made of sugar,
   but they looked like jewels.
   Most people didn't try to eat them,
   though I'm sure you could.

"Nevertheless,

when Wendy Wallerstein tried,

it turned out she couldn't.

Wendy's parents and ours were friends.

The Wallersteins lived in a fancy apartment,

overlooking a park.

Wendy was a somewhat

overdressed child

who loved to eat.

She came to

your father's party

in a lacy white dress

and pinafore,

with a lacy white slip

underneath,

lacy white tights,

and black patent-leather Mary Jane shoes.

"'Ooooh!' Wendy said

when she saw the cake.

'Look at all those silver beads.'

Well, naturally then,

when Grandma sliced the cake,

she put quite a few of the beads

on Wendy's plate.

I still can hear Wendy say,

'I love silver beads.

I love to wear them,

and I love to eat them, too.'

"Unfortunately, Wendy was eating them
at the same time she said it.
She swallowed wrong.
At least one silver bead
went down her windpipe,
stuck there, and choked her.
Her eyes got wide. She couldn't talk
or even make a sound."

"Did she almost die?" I ask.
"Not quite," says Aunt Rose.
"She pointed at her neck.

"Grandpa saw right away
what was happening.
He knew what to do.
He scooped Wendy up,
turned her over,
and hit her on her back.

"Silver beads popped out of her mouth,
along with some half-eaten cake.

"Then Grandpa turned Wendy right side up
   and stood her on the floor.
   Her face was red as a tomato,
   and not only from the choking.
   'I have to go home now,'
   Wendy kept saying,
   until finally Grandma called
   Wendy's mother to come get her."

"Was the party ruined?" I ask.

"Not really," says Aunt Rose.

"Well, no one cared for
   any more cake after that,
   but we all played musical chairs
   and pin the tail on the donkey,
   and everyone had a very good time.
   Except, I guess, for Wendy."

"I see," I say.

   Then I kiss Girl,
   and everyone, good-bye.

When I get home,

Pop is waiting for me.

We have fish and rice for supper.

Just as we finish eating,

the telephone rings.

It's Uncle Leo.

"Hi, Harry," he says.

"Your Aunt Rose and I

were just discussing your party.

We have a surprise for you."

"Yes?" I say. I think,

probably they are getting me

a cowboy hat for a present.

Or else maybe a clown for my party.

Before I can ask which, Uncle Leo says,

"Both of us are coming,

and we'll also be your entertainment.

Aunt Rose will play her portable piano,

and I will play my tuba."

I certainly am surprised to hear this.

"Thank you," I tell him.

The next day I walk home from school
with Eddie and Dorcas.
"I'm having live music
at my birthday party," I tell them.
"My aunt and uncle are coming
with their portable piano and tuba."
"Wow," says Eddie. "Maybe I
could bring my drums."
Eddie has been taking drum lessons
since kindergarten.

"I guess that means no clown,"
　says Dorcas. "Well, at least now
　Girl has a way to come to your party."
"Right," I say.
　Then we all wave good-bye,
　and I turn onto my block.
　I hurry the rest of the way.
　My father worries if I'm late.
　Also, today is the day we order
　my cake and buy party supplies.
"Hi, Harry. Are you ready to go?"
　my father says as soon as he sees me.
　We get into the car and ride downtown.

We look at pictures of cakes
in the bakery. I pick out one
in the shape of a cowboy hat.
"I want chocolate cake
and chocolate icing, please,"
I tell the baker.
"Right," she says.
"Also, please write,
'Happy Birthday, Harry,'
on the brim," my father adds.

Next we go to the party store.
I pick out matching cowboy plates
and cups, party hats, a tablecloth,
and invitations. Also, plastic spoons
and forks, balloons, games and prizes,
and birthday candles.
"Are you planning a rodeo?"
the salesclerk asks,
ringing up our order.

"Oh, no, a birthday party," I tell her.

"But I'm hoping for a cowboy hat."

"I see. Good luck," she says as we leave.

"Thank you," I say.

When we get home, my father and I
write out the invitations.

We stamp and mail them.

I cross my fingers and make a wish:

Please let someone give me
a cowboy hat for a present.

Saturday, before my party begins,
Aunt Rose, Uncle Leo, and Girl
arrive with the piano and tuba.
Girl has on a fancy new collar,
red with rhinestones.

My father sees her and starts sneezing.
He sneezes for most of the party.

The guests begin arriving.

"Happy birthday, Harry," they say,

handing me presents.

"You can open them later,"

Pop says, and takes them inside.

Aunt Rose and Uncle Leo play music.

Guests are taking off sweaters,

tapping their feet, bobbing their heads.

Edith and Edna start dancing.

"Time to come to the table,"
Pop says.
"Happy birthday to you . . ."
play the tuba and piano.
Pop brings in the cake.
"Ooooh! It's a cowboy hat,"
everyone says, seeing its shape.
Pop lights the candles.

Everyone sings "Happy Birthday,"
except for Uncle Leo,
who is still blowing.

"Make a wish," my father says.

I close my eyes.

Please let one of my presents

be a cowboy hat.

Then I blow out all the candles

in one breath. Everyone claps.

I slice the first slice;

then Pop cuts the rest.

Aunt Rose and Uncle Leo scoop ice cream,

pour fruit punch, help serve.

Afterward we play games.

Dorcas wins pin the tail on the donkey.

"I think she could see," Edith whispers.

"I could not, either," says Dorcas.

Uncle Leo plays the tuba
for musical chairs. Barry wins.

"I would have won, except
he tripped me," says Edna.

"Time to open the presents,"

my father says, carrying them in.

I sit on the floor, with everyone else

in a circle around me.

"Open mine first,"

say some of the guests.

"Don't open mine first," say the rest.

Pop hands me a present from the top.

"That's mine," says Eddie.

I take off the paper and open the box.

Inside is a red cowboy hat

with a black band all around it

and cords that hang down

to tie under my chin.

I try it on. It fits perfectly.

"Thank you," I say.

"It's just what I wanted."

"I know," says Eddie.

I open my next present.

"That's mine," says José.

I take out a black cowboy hat

with a red band all around it

and cords that hang down

to tie under my chin.

I try it on. It fits perfectly, too.

"Thank you," I say.

"It's just what I wanted."

"I know," says José.

My next present is from Edith.
It is a white cowboy hat
with a matching band
and cords that hang down
to tie under my chin.
"Thank you," I say.
"It's just what I wanted."
I try hard to sound sincere.
"I thought so," says Edith.
By the time I have opened
all my presents, I have
seven cowboy hats, including
a ten-gallon one from my father.

I also have: a pair of cowboy boots
from Aunt Rose and Uncle Leo,
a book on juggling from Dorcas,
a baseball cap and bat
from Barry and Edna,
and a dozen gingerbread people.
"My mom forgot to buy something,
so she baked instead," says Martin.
"I hope you like them."
"Oh, I do," I tell him.

Just then Aunt Rose holds up
a brown paper bag that isn't a present.
"Face paint," she says, taking it out.
She and Uncle Leo
paint clown faces on everyone,
except for Girl and my father.

Girl goes under the table and watches.
"I think I'm allergic to face paint,"
Pop says.

Parents begin arriving

to pick up their children.

"Thank you for coming," I tell everyone.

"Thank you for inviting me,"

everyone says.

Eddie's mom fingers the tuba.

"I always wanted to play one,"

she tells Uncle Leo.

"It's never too late to start," he says.

My father is sneezing harder than ever.

"Are you coming down with a cold?"

parents keep asking.

"An allergy," my father answers.

"I have an allergy."

He rolls his eyes at Girl.

His eyes are red.

After all the guests have left
and we have straightened the house,
Uncle Leo says,
"What interesting presents.
Harry could open a hat store."
"Sure he could,"
Aunt Rose says, smiling.
"But if I had so many nice hats,
I'd hang them all on my wall
for decoration.
Well, except for the one I was wearing."
"What a good idea!" my father says.
I think so, too.

So that's what we do.

Pop gets a hammer, nails, hooks,

and a tape measure

from the basement.

Uncle Leo measures the wall and

pencils X's in all the right places.

Aunt Rose holds up the hooks

and bangs in the nails.

Then I stand on my step stool
and hang all my hats in a circle,
except for the one I am wearing.
"I think they look very nice
hanging there," I say.
"Sure they do," says Uncle Leo.

Then he and Aunt Rose kiss me good-bye.
Girl kisses me, too,
and they all go home together.

"Happy birthday, Harry,"
   my father says a little later,
   tucking me into bed.
   He kisses me good-night
   and turns out the light.
"Good night," I say.
   I still can see my hats
   hanging on the wall.
   I lie in bed and
   think about my birthday.
   My party turned out fine.
   Everyone had a good time.
   My cake didn't slip,
   no one got sick,
   unless you count Pop's allergy,
   plus I got such good presents.

I count my hats,

then plan what I will do tomorrow.

First I will practice juggling.

Next I will play baseball

with my father.

Then we'll come inside for juice

and gingerbread people.

After that I will put on
my cowboy boots and
ten-gallon hat, get Girl,
and take her for a walk.

Maybe we will walk back here
to see my hat collection.
I think this was the
best birthday, ever,
in my life.
At least
so far.

BARBARA ANN PORTE's popular "Harry" books for beginning readers include <u>Harry's Visit</u>, <u>Harry's Dog</u>, <u>Harry's Mom</u>, <u>Harry in Trouble</u>, and <u>Harry Gets an Uncle</u>. For young readers she has also written <u>"Leave That Cricket Be, Alan Lee"</u> and three books about Abigail and Sam, their parents, and Benton, their dog: <u>A Turkey Drive and Other Tales</u>, <u>Taxicab Tales</u>, and <u>The Take-Along Dog</u>.

YOSSI ABOLAFIA was born in Israel. He is the author-artist of <u>Fox Tale</u>, <u>My Three Uncles</u>, <u>Yanosh's Island</u>, and <u>A Fish for Mrs. Gardenia</u>. Among the many books he has illustrated are Barbara Ann Porte's "Harry" books, <u>Ten Old Pails</u> by Nicholas Heller, <u>Stop, Thief!</u> by Robert Kalan, and <u>Am I Beautiful?</u> by Else Holmelund Minarik. He lives with his wife and children near Jerusalem.